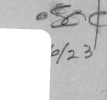
MW00912042

6/23

Rachel's Library

RICHARD UNGAR

TOPEKA & SHAWNEE CO.
PUBLIC LIBRARY
TOPEKA, KANSAS

Published in Canada by Tundra Books,
481 University Avenue, Toronto, Ontario M5G 2E9

Published in the United States by Tundra Books of Northern New York,
P.O. Box 1030, Plattsburgh, New York 12901

Library of Congress Control Number: 2004100580

National Library of Canada Cataloguing in Publication

Ungar, Richard
Rachel's library / Richard Ungar.

For ages 7-10.
ISBN 0-88776-678-1

I. Title.

PS8591.N42R42 2004   jC813'.6   C2004-900495-6

We acknowledge the financial support of the Government of Canada through the
Book Publishing Industry Development Program (BPIDP) and that of the Government
of Ontario through the Ontario Media Development Corporation's Ontario Book
Initiative. We further acknowledge the support of the Canada Council for the Arts
and the Ontario Arts Council for our publishing program.

This book was inspired by the story "Chelm's School"
by Samuel Tenenbaum (1902-).

Medium: watercolor and colored pencil on paper

Printed in Hong Kong, China

1 2 3 4 5 6   09 08 07 06 05 04

For my parents

"People of Chelm, we have a serious problem!" Simon the Carpenter announced to the villagers gathered in the square. "Yesterday, a traveler from Minsk asked me whether it's true that we eat breakfast for dinner and dinner for breakfast. When I replied, 'Of course,' he laughed. And that is not all. Just this morning I overheard a porter from Lublin saying to another: 'Those people of Chelm are so foolish, they wear socks on their hands and gloves on their feet!'"

"But, Simon," said Izzie the Water-Carrier, "what is the problem? After all, it is true . . . at least in winter."

"True or not," replied Simon, "we must put an end to outsiders regarding us as foolish!"

All of the villagers nodded. But how could they convince people of their true wisdom? After much debate, they decided to send a special delegation to Warsaw. After all, they reasoned, in a place as worldly as Warsaw, they were bound to find a solution.

As with all other decisions of importance in Chelm, the adults were asked to draw straws to see who would go. Simon dazzled everyone with a very bold straw drawing. The drawings made by Izzie and Myriam the Matchmaker were equally impressive. In short order, Simon, Izzie, and Myriam were chosen as Chelm's special delegation.

Early the next morning, the special delegation set out for Warsaw. As they bumped along in Izzie's cart, Simon noticed the blanket beside him jiggle. *Nothing more than a rough patch of road*, he thought. But a moment later, he heard a sneeze. It came from underneath the blanket. Simon grabbed a corner and flung it upwards.

"Rachel?"

"Hello, Father. A perfect day for a trip to Warsaw, isn't it?"

"But you can't . . . I mean . . . aren't you supposed to be helping your mother?" said Simon.

"Mama doesn't need me today. But don't worry, Father, I will not be any trouble. I have brought along something to occupy me for the journey." Rachel pulled a book out of the folds of the blanket and held it up. The title was: *Detective Deborah and the Mysterious Case of the Pickled Herring*.

Simon frowned. "Very well, Rachel, since you are here, you may come along. But remember, this is a business trip. There will be no stops at the candy shop on Lubelski Street."

"Oh, thank you, Father!" Rachel hugged Simon and then plunged back into the world of Detective Deborah.

After traveling all morning and most of the afternoon, the dusty group finally arrived in Warsaw. The city was bustling: old and young, porters, peddlers, and scholars talking, laughing, and shouting as they went about their business.

Izzie navigated the cart down a broad avenue. Gazing up at the grand buildings, he remarked, "Look, everyone! The houses here are so tall! Even a bird would be out of breath flying so high! I am certain if we built houses like these in Chelm, no one would ever doubt our wisdom."

"But who would want to live in such houses?" said Myriam. "Not I, for one. From such a height I would never be able to peek into Sarah the Weaver's parlor to see what's going on, or smell the wonderful aroma coming from Selma the Cook's kitchen."

Myriam was right, they agreed. And so they carried on. . . .

After a while, the avenue narrowed and the buildings were replaced with fine shops. A gentleman sporting a top hat, handsome overcoat, and shiny boots emerged from one of the shops.

"Look at that fine fellow!" Izzie exclaimed. "I am certain that if everyone in Chelm dressed as stylishly as him, no one would think us foolish."

"But, Izzie," remarked Simon, "what can you do with a top hat? You cannot easily toss it onto a hook or warm your hands inside it, as you can my wool cap! And with all the wonderful mud puddles in Chelm, no one would ever have shiny boots for long."

Simon was right, they agreed. And so they carried on. . . .

Soon they arrived at a busy marketplace. All manner of scent and spice filled their nostrils.

"I have it!" declared Myriam. "Do you see how that vendor is using a scale to weigh his fish? I am certain that if Chelm had a scale like that, everyone would think us very wise."

"But, Myriam," said Izzie, "what is the use? No fish from Chelm would ever agree to be placed on a scale. They much prefer swimming in the river."

Izzie was right, they agreed. And so they carried on. . . .

By now the sun was low in the sky. Simon, Izzie, and Myriam knew that it was time to begin the journey back to Chelm. But they were reluctant to return empty-handed. And so, unable to decide whether to carry on or turn back, the delegation halted.

When Rachel saw where they had stopped, she leaped from the cart. "Father, I know this place." She pointed to a building with an elegant door. "I have been here before with Mama. It is a library!"

"A what?"

"A library, Father. A place of many books."

"So? What can such a place do for us?" asked Simon.

"Everything!" replied Rachel. "Think, Father. Who is the wisest person in all of Chelm?"

"Our Rebbe, of course," Simon answered, without hesitation.

"And what is our Rebbe always doing – that is, when he is not helping others or in synagogue, praying?"

Simon was baffled for a moment, but when he saw two scholars walking by, an idea suddenly came to him. "He reads his books!"

"Exactly!" said Rachel. "So what better way can there be to show the world that we are wise than by having our very own library in Chelm!"

And with that, Rachel bounded up the step and disappeared into the building.

Simon, Izzie, and Myriam quietly considered Rachel's idea. *A library for Chelm!* No one could think of a single thing wrong with it. A few moments later Rachel emerged, clutching a slim volume.

Simon squinted at the title: *The Collected Writings of the Sages of Chelm.* "But what about the rest?" he said. "One skinny book is hardly enough. We need all of the books in that library to take back with us to Chelm!"

"But, Father, if we took all the books, the people of Warsaw would be left with nothing to read. Trust me. I am certain that one borrowed book will be enough to start."

Simon frowned, but there was no time to argue. The sun was beginning to set and they had a long journey ahead.

Dawn was breaking when they finally arrived back in Chelm. Despite the early hour, all the villagers were in the square to greet them.

"Nu?" said Hershel the Tailor, spying the empty cart. "Where is the thing that will convince all who travel through Chelm that we are wise and not foolish?"

"Show them, Rachel," Simon said.

Rachel took the book that she had borrowed from the Warsaw Library and stood it up on a crate next to the village water pump.

Everyone stared at the book. *Surely there must be something magical about it,* they thought. *Why else would the special delegation have brought it back from Warsaw?* No one blinked for fear of missing a miracle.

After a while Simon whispered, "Rachel, people are beginning to lose patience. They are saying we have failed. They are asking what good is a single book on a crate!"

"You are right, Father. Something needs to be done."

Rachel ran home and retrieved her favorite book. Then she approached the crate and, very deliberately, placed it next to the volume already there. Suddenly, it was as if a spell had been broken. . . .

"I too have a book that I have finished reading," exclaimed Sarah the Weaver.

"And I can donate a book also," shouted Hershel the Tailor.

"And I as well!" chimed in Rafael the Musician.

"We will need shelves to hold our books," declared Simon, sprinting off to his workshop to build them.

"And don't forget walls and a roof," called Izzie, running to catch up to Simon.

Soon the square was alive with villagers hurrying this way and that. Some placed books on the new shelves. Others put up the walls. Still others brought chairs and tables.

The villagers were so pleased with their new library, which they named Rachel's Library, that it was not unusual for them to make daily trips there to borrow books. In fact, some of the villagers, Izzie the Water-Carrier included, found themselves making at least three trips there each day. Not always to borrow books, mind you. More often, it was to pump water from the village water pump, which, after all the dust had settled, was now located squarely within the walls of Rachel's Library.